THE
D U N E ™
STORYBOOK

THE

DUNE™

STORYBOOK

Joan D. Vinge

Adapted from a screenplay by David Lynch

Based on the novel by Frank Herbert

G. P. PUTNAM'S SONS

NEW YORK

The Dune Storybook by Joan D. Vinge. Adapted from a screenplay by David Lynch.
Based on the novel by Frank Herbert. Design by Bernard Schleifer.
Copyright © 1984 by Dino De Laurentiis Corporation. All rights reserved,
which includes the right to reproduce this book or portions thereof in any form whatsoever.
Published in the United States by G. P. Putnam's Sons.
Published simultaneously in Canada by General Publishing Co. Limited, Toronto.

Library of Congress Cataloging in Publication Data
Vinge, Joan D.   The Dune storybook.
Summary: Young Paul Atreides, son of a powerful family from the planet Caladan, may be the looked-for
leader who will save the desert planet Dune, source of a precious spice which gives people strange
mental powers. [1. Science fiction] I. Title. PS3572.I53D8   1984   813'.54   [Fic]   84-8250   ISBN 0-399-12949-9
Printed in the United States of America.
TM: A trademark of Dino De Laurentiis Corporation and licensed
by Merchandising Corporation of America, Inc.

THE GREAT GALACTIC EMPIRE had lasted for thousands of years. Its Emperor, Shaddam IV, believed it would last forever. He was wrong. In a far corner of the Empire was a desert planet called Dune. It was the most important planet in the Empire, because it was the only planet on which the spice melange could be found. Melange could give people strange mental powers. The Fremen, people who lived on Dune, hated the Empire, because it ruled their world harshly. Their legends said that someday a great leader would come to their world. He would set their world free, and change the galaxy forever. They were right. This is the story of how it happened.

FAR ACROSS THE GALAXY from Dune lay a world called Caladan. On Caladan, great waves were rolling like black glass through a night filled with wind and rain. They crashed against the rugged cliff below Castle Caladan, a palace-fortress that looked as ancient as the stone on which it sat. It was the home of the Atreides family. The Atreides were one of the most powerful families in the Empire. They were in a long-standing feud with another powerful family, the Harkonnens. Now, the Emperor was going to trick the Atreides family into fighting the Harkonnens over who would control the spice mining on Dune.

Inside the castle, young Paul Atreides sat in a warm, bright training room. He was a dark-haired, handsome boy of fifteen. He wore a fine uniform, the clothing of a noble, because he was the son of Duke Leto Atreides. Someday he would be the Duke himself. Now he was studying filmbooks and maps of the world Dune. He knew that he and his family would be leaving for Dune tomorrow. *"Arrakis" means "dune" in the language of the Fremen,* he thought. Arrakis was what the natives called their world. *Sand dune.* The filmbook filled his eyes with a changing three-dimensional view of his new home. It was a world of great deserts, orange and brown and silver.

He heard footsteps in the hallway outside his room, coming toward his door. Three men entered the room behind him. He knew who they were without turning to look at them: Thufir Hawat, his father's Mentat, whose special training and use of the spice melange made him a kind of human computer. Gurney Halleck, his father's weapons master, who was also a poet. And Dr. Yueh, his private tutor and his father's loyal physician. The three men had been his special teachers since he was very young. Thufir Hawat cleared his throat.

"I know, Thufir," Paul said. He turned around. "I was sitting with my back to the door. But I heard you all coming down the hall. My father sent you here to test me again . . . but I'm not in the mood tonight."

The Mentat frowned.

"Not in the mood?" Gurney Halleck said angrily. "Mood's a thing for young lovers—it's not for fighters!" He switched on his body shield and drew his knife.

Paul leaped to his feet, snapping on his own protective force field. He drew his knife. Gurney leaped forward, attacking him furiously. Their energy shields crackled loudly as they touched. Paul struck and parried with his blade, surprised and almost frightened. His teacher had never attacked him this hard before.

The fight carried them around the room, until at last Paul managed to pin Gurney against a table top. His knife pressed his teacher's throat.

"Good, the slow blade used with control and discipline penetrates the shield," Gurney said breathlessly. "But look down."

Paul looked down, and saw Gurney's blade touching his body.

"We'd have died together. But I guess you were in the 'mood' after all." Gurney smiled grimly.

Paul stepped back and turned off his shield. "Would you really have stabbed me?"

Gurney nodded. "If you hadn't fought your best, I would have scratched you a good one."

Paul sighed. "Things are so serious around here lately."

"Tomorrow we go to Dune," Gurney said. "Dune is dangerous, and so are our rivals, the Harkonnens. We know they won't give up their control of the spice mining on Dune as easily as it appears that they have."

"You think this is a trap for us?" Paul asked. "Then why are we going?"

"We have our new army . . . and our new secret weapon. And a trap is only a trap if you don't expect it."

The three men and the boy looked at one another for a long moment. Finally Thufir said, "Let's get on with the testing."

Gurney made certain no one else was in the room, and then he locked the door. The weapon they were about to test was a closely guarded secret of the Atreides family.

A fighter robot was lowered from the ceiling. It was a frightening, deadly machine, covered with sharp knives and spines that could cut a man to pieces very quickly. It came alive as it floated above the floor; its blades seemed to move faster than the eye could follow. Quickly Dr. Yueh placed a collar with the special voice box called a weirding module around Paul's neck.

Paul circled the robot cautiously, leaping away from its weapons. His face was stiff with tension. He followed a plan that Gurney had made him practice over and over. If he made one mistake, he might be badly hurt. Suddenly, at the perfect moment, Paul ran at the robot, shouting. A terrible roar came through the weirding box he wore. Paul kept shouting, moving his hands in a secret pattern while holding his sound gun in his right hand. The robot jerked to a stop and burst into flames.

"That was perfect!" Gurney whispered to Dr. Yueh. All three men knew that Paul was something special. He was the best student they had ever taught. But he would need every skill they had taught him, on the world called Dune.

AT THE SAME MOMENT, deep in the heart of the Empire, the lights of the landing field burned brightly in front of the Emperor's palace. A Guild ship came down out of the night and landed before the glorious, golden building. Inside the palace, the Galactic Emperor, Shaddam IV, waited alone in a golden-walled chamber. A Third-Stage Guildsman was coming to see him in secret. The Emperor was sure that this meeting would mean trouble.

The ancient, mysterious Spacing Guild was very powerful. It controlled all space travel in his Empire. He knew Guild members used the spice melange, which allowed them to "fold space" with their minds, and guide their ships between the stars. The spice made space travel possible. It also gave the Guildsmen rare mental abilities. Sometimes they could see into the future—and perhaps even into the Emperor's own mind.

Fifty Guildsmen entered the Emperor's chamber, bringing a huge black box with them. Inside the box, in a glass tank, the Third-Stage Navigator drifted. He barely looked human. For centuries the Guild had experimented to change human genes so that Navigators could "fold space." A Third-Stage Navigator was changed so much from a normal human being that he could not live outside his tank. His body was so distorted that it looked like the body of a giant grasshopper. He swam toward the Emperor and raised his great fleshy head. His eyes were totally deep blue. He spoke through a translator machine.

"Is there a problem?" the Emperor asked him nervously. "Usually you only visit when there is a problem."

The Navigator did not answer for a long moment. Then he said, "Your thoughts are transparent. I see plans within plans. I see two Great Houses—House Atreides and House Harkonnen—feuding. I see you behind it. You must tell us about it."

"The Atreides are building a secret army," the Emperor said. "And the Duke is becoming too popular with the other Great Houses of the Empire. I know he has a secret weapon that uses sound to destroy things. He could be a threat to me. I have ordered Duke Atreides to go to the planet Dune, where the spice melange is found. His people will take over and mine the spice, replacing their enemies the Harkonnens. The Atreides think this is a victory for them. They think it will give them great power. But once they are on Dune, Baron Harkonnen will return and make a sneak attack on them. He will get rid of the Atreides for me. I have promised him five legions of my Sardaukar terror troops."

The Navigator thrashed violently in his tank.

The Emperor said quickly, "I would never put your supply of melange in danger! Without it, you would not be able to fold space, and my Empire would become separate, unreachable planets again. I promise you, the mining of spice on Dune will not be interrupted."

The Navigator grew quiet again. His mind looked into the future to see what would happen with the Emperor's plot. "There is one small problem I can see with your plan," he said at last. "You must make sure that Paul, the son of Duke Leto Atreides, is killed with his father. Then your plan will be one that we like. . . . I didn't say this to you." The box began to close, hiding the Navigator from sight. "I was never here," he whispered.

"I understand." The Emperor nodded. He watched the Guildsmen leave the room, and he frowned. "Why would they want the Duke's *son* killed?" he asked himself.

B ACK ON CALADAN, the night moved on toward morning. Duke Leto's son, Paul, slept, never suspecting what the Emperor planned. Instead he had strange dreams of Arrakis, Dune, the desert world: He dreamed of water dripping into a vast, dark lake . . . of a beautiful girl who said, "Tell me of your homeworld, Usul."

Paul stirred restlessly, and woke. He heard footsteps outside his door. His mother, the proud, elegant, copper-haired Lady Jessica, stood in the doorway with an old woman he did not know. He closed his eyes, pretending to be asleep.

The stranger whispered, "The Emperor has begun a plot we cannot stop. We'll save what we can . . . *but for the father, nothing!*"

His mother stared at the old woman, and her face filled with grief. "Why must this happen?"

"You were told to have a daughter, not a son," the woman said. "You know our plans must be carried out exactly. But you disobeyed me. You ruined cen-

turies of genetic planning. Did you really think your son would be the Kwisatz Haderach? How dare you!"

"I felt it could happen," Jessica murmured. "And Leto wanted a son so much . . ."

"Indeed!" the stranger said scornfully. "You thought only of him? What other people want has nothing to do with this! An Atreides daughter could have been married to a Harkonnen son, and healed the feud between the families. That was our plan. Did you think you knew more than ninety generations of the Bene Gesserit? You were my greatest student . . . and you are my greatest disappointment." She looked at Paul suddenly. "He's awake! He's listening to us. Good—he should be sly. Paul Atreides, I want to see you in your mother's chambers. Get up and get ready." She turned and walked away.

Jessica called softly, "Paul? This is very important. Hurry."

Paul got up and dressed, half curious and half worried. He went to his mother's rooms. Dim light from a glowglobe shone on the faces of his mother and the stranger. "Paul, this is the Reverend Mother Helen Mohiam," Jessica said. "She is an advisor to the Emperor." Paul saw the other woman clearly for the first time. Her wrinkled, ancient body was hidden beneath heavy black robes. Her head was shaved beneath her hood, and her teeth were made of metal. He guessed that this old woman must be an important member of the Bene Gesserit.

The Bene Gesserit order was an ancient school of mental and physical training that his mother belonged to. He knew the order held great secrets, just as the Spacing Guild did. Its members could look into the future by using the spice melange, like the Guild did. They used their influence to affect the way human history would turn out. The Reverend Mother Mohiam gave advice to the Emperor; but she did it to serve her own order and its secret plans. Only

women became Bene Gesserit, but his mother had taught him many of their
ways. "The Reverend Mother is going to . . . observe you." Jessica glanced
nervously at the old woman. "Listen to the Reverend Mother, Paul . . . please
listen, and do what she tells you."

Paul watched her leave the room. He wondered why she looked so frightened, and why this was happening to him.

"COME HERE," the Reverend Mother ordered. She used The Voice, a Bene
Gesserit skill that forced the listener to do anything she asked.

"No." Paul fought her power, but he couldn't resist it. He moved toward
her.

The Reverend Mother held out a green metal cube.

"Put your right hand in this box," she said.

"What's in it?" Paul asked, as he obeyed.

"Pain."

Paul jerked back. But then he saw the glint of a needle in the old woman's
hand.

"STOP!" she commanded. "I hold at your neck the gom jabbar. It is a
poisoned needle—but it kills only animals."

"Are you saying the Duke's son is an animal?" Paul asked angrily.

"I am saying you may be human," she answered. "Your animal instincts
will tell you to pull your hand out of the box when you feel the pain. But if you
are a real human being you will be able to control your instincts. If you can't,
then you are an animal, and you will die. Do you feel the pain starting?"

Paul nodded. "It burns," he whispered. Suddenly he was very much afraid.
I must not fear, he thought desperately, repeating words his mother had taught
him. *Fear is the mind-killer. I will let it pass over me and through me.* He felt the skin
on his hand beginning to blister. The pain grew worse and worse. He was sure

that his hand must be burning away to nothing. But he could not move or he would die. He clenched his other fist and bit his lip, but at last he could not keep from crying out. *"The pain!"*

"No! Enough!" the Reverend Mother said to herself. "No woman child ever withstood that much. I must have wanted you to fail. Take your hand out of the box and look at it, *young human*. Do it!"

Paul pulled his hand from the box. He was afraid to look, but when he did he stared in amazement. There was no sign of any burn.

"The pain was caused by stimulating your nerves," the Reverend Mother explained. "A human can resist any pain. This was a test of your courage in a crisis."

Paul took a deep breath. "I understand, now," he said.

The Reverend Mother stared at him. She touched his forehead for a moment, as if she were reading his thoughts. "Perhaps you are the Kwisatz Haderach," she murmured.

"What is that?" Paul asked.

"The first male Bene Gesserit. The one who sees across all space and time. The one who will take the Water of Life—the Truthsayer drug—and see things none of us have ever seen. He will go where we cannot. Many men have tried . . . and died. Jessica!" she called.

His mother came quickly into the room. Her face filled with relief as she saw him.

"Jessica, you must teach your son The Voice. He will need it for his safety on Dune."

"What about my father's safety?" Paul asked. "I heard you talking as if he was dead. He isn't!" Jessica caught Paul's arm, holding him back, as he reached for the Reverend Mother. "Tell me he won't die! Mother! Tell me!"

"What can be done has been done," the Reverend Mother said. She covered her head and walked toward the door.

Jessica watched the Reverend Mother leave the room, and tears filled her eyes.

Later that night, Jessica entered Duke Leto's study. He looked up from his desk, smiling. As she saw his face, love for him filled her heart. Love had made her give him the son he had wanted, instead of the daughter she had been told to have. But even her love could not change the future that the Reverend Mother had warned her about. The tears she had been holding back for hours suddenly began to fall.

"Jessica! What is it?" The Duke stood and took her in his arms.

She looked away from his eyes as her grief filled her. She couldn't tell him the truth, and so she only said, "I'll miss Caladan so much." She wept harder.

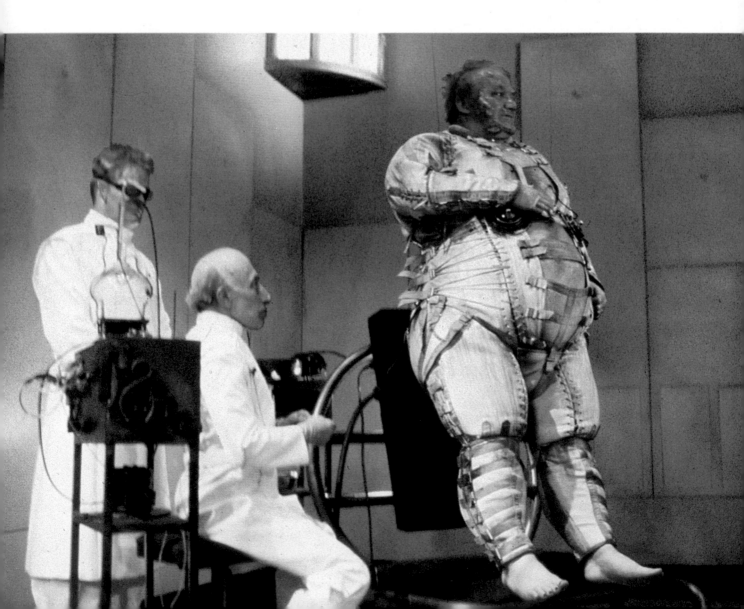

FAR ACROSS THE GALAXY from Caladan lay Giedi Prime, a world of darkness and despair. It was the homeworld of the Harkonnens, the deadly enemies of Paul's family. The surface of the planet was a vast, oozing sea of oil. The city in which the Harkonnens lived was a gigantic box of black steel over one hundred stories high, floating on the oily sea. Millions of electrical cables bristled from its surface, feeding from energy taps high in the air. Ringing the city were rows of roaring furnaces. Their chimneys were capped with nightmarish metal faces. Foul smoke billowed from their mouths.

In the city of steel and smoke, the corrupt Baron Harkonnen sat in a green porcelain room with his Mentat Piter and his favorite nephews, Feyd and Rabban. The Baron was a monstrous figure. His grossly fat body festered with sickness caused by long years of evil habits. His great weight was held up by antigravity suspensors that floated him above the floor. "Tell them, Piter!" he said. "Tell my nephews about my plan to destroy my enemies, the Atreides."

"Sir . . . are you sure I should?" Piter asked.

"Tell them!" the Baron ordered. "They will have their place in it."

Piter explained the trap that had been laid for Paul's family on Dune. The Baron smiled wickedly as he thought of the key to his plan's success. He had forced one of Duke Leto's most trusted advisors to become a traitor. The Duke would expect a Harkonnen attack, but he would never suspect his friends to betray him. This trap couldn't fail.

As the Baron gloated over his coming victory, Paul and his family left Caladan for the last time. More than three thousand Atreides spaceships rose gracefully into orbit from the planet's surface. They entered a waiting Guild Heighliner. The Heighliner was so immense that it made the other ships look like a swarm of insects. The Atreides ships would only be a small part of its cargo.

In the Heighliner's control room, a Navigator emerged from a tunnel into a vast room filled with orange spice gas. He entered a huge, many-dimensional map of the universe. Using his strange powers, he began to fold space, changing the shape of the galaxy. He rearranged the places of Caladan and Dune in the map; for a moment he tore holes in the very heart of the galaxy. Stars were blown about like sparks in the wind. Lightning flashed around Dune, and thunder echoed. The Navigator dove deep into the widening rings of light. He followed the world Dune into other dimensions until he disappeared.

Suddenly the Heighliner burst out of nothingness into orbit above Dune. It was back in the universe its passengers knew, after a trip through hyperspace. The three thousand ships of the Atreides roared down to a landing on the hot, barren surface of their new homeworld.

Arrakeen Palace lay in the brownish-orange haze of the dusty Arrakeen Valley. As Paul and his family left their ship, their new subjects greeted them with pageantry and shouting. The Harkonnens had been hated tyrants who had caused much suffering on Dune. The people were celebrating because they were gone. They were not celebrating because the new Duke had come. Duke Leto knew that he would have to show the people of Dune that he was a better ruler than Baron Harkonnen. Otherwise, he would never win their loyalty for his House.

Paul entered Arrakeen Palace with his parents, as the Atreides flag was raised overhead. Thick stone walls kept the interior cool and dark, even in the blinding heat of afternoon. Much of the palace was underground.

Atreides troops and servants began the enormous job of unpacking belongings and making their new palace safe from Harkonnen sabotage. Several Harkonnen booby traps and spy devices had already been found. The Duke knew the Harkonnens would not give up Dune willingly. He feared some kind of Harkonnen treachery. But he knew he could trust his people. If they were careful, he thought his family would be safe and secure.

Meanwhile, Paul explored his new home. He wandered through the shadowy stone hallways of Arrakeen Palace for hours. Tiles covered the walls in strange decorations, like patterns of stars. He could hear the troops and the household staff all around him. Outside, he could hear the cries of watersellers in the streets around the palace. Everywhere there were reminders of how precious water was here. This new world interested him very much, but he still felt uneasy. The dusty gloom of the palace's endless buried halls depressed him. He could not forget the warnings about Dune and his father that he had heard back on Caladan.

Paul reached his bedroom at last. He decided to take a rest, and study his tapes some more. As he went into the room he saw a tray of pastries. He took one and bit into it. He looked at it in surprise, as a flavor like cinnamon filled his mouth. "Spice," he murmured. Here on Dune, which was the world melange came from, the spice was in everything. He went on eating, curious, looking out the window. All at once the light from the window seemed to glow white-hot. In its heart he began to see visions. He saw a Guild Navigator . . . he saw himself, lying in the desert as if he were dead . . . he saw Arrakeen Palace in flames.

All his life he had had strange dreams—and some of them had come true. He had always known which ones would, but he had never known why. Now he could feel that he had been meant to come to Dune. His destiny lay here. Suddenly he knew that his life had a terrible purpose. But he could not see what it was—yet.

Paul stood trembling as the visions faded. He turned back, wanting to lie down on his bed. But as he turned, he saw a silvery metal dart float silently out of the bed's headboard. *A hunter-seeker!* Paul froze. He knew that the poisoned dart would kill him if he moved. If he stood still, it might not find him in the darkened room. His mind raced, trying to find a way out of this deadly trap.

Just then the door to his room opened. The hunter-seeker shot past Paul toward the motion. As it passed, he reached out and grabbed it. It buzzed and twisted violently in his hand as he smashed it against the wall.

Looking back at its target, he saw the Shadout Mapes, the palace's native housekeeper. Her eyes were entirely blue, like all the natives' eyes were.

"You saved my life," she whispered, shaken. "We Fremen pay our debts—I tell you now, there is a *traitor* in your house." She turned, and ran off down the hall.

"A Fremen!" Paul whispered. The Fremen lived in the great deserts of Dune. They were a mysterious people. Only a few of them lived in the towns near the palace. No one even knew how many Fremen there really were. But Paul knew they were supposed to hate the offworlders who controlled their planet. There were rumors of a Fremen rebellion. Hastily he buckled on his shield belt and activated the field.

His mother came into the room. "Is something wrong?" she asked.

"There's a traitor among us," he said quietly. "We should warn father."

His mother looked away, unable to hide the fear in her eyes. "I wish we'd never come here," she said. But she knew there was no way she could have stopped it.

J ESSICA SAT ALONE in her room, wondering what to do. She could not guess who the traitor might be. She could only hope that Leto's search would find out who it was in time.

She looked up from her table as the palace housekeeper entered the room. "Yes?"

"I am the Shadout Mapes," the woman said. "What are your orders, my lady?"

"Shadout," Jessica murmured, almost to herself. "That's an ancient word."

"You know the ancient languages of Arrakis?" the woman asked.

Jessica nodded.

"As the legend says," Mapes whispered.

Jessica knew that the Bene Gesserit order had visited this world long ago, to spread its teachings. Its missionaries had spread stories about the wisdom and powers of its members on all the worlds of the Empire. Those stories became local legends, which would protect a Bene Gesserit if she ever needed help. Jessica knew that she must encourage the native woman's belief. "I know the Dark things and the way of the Great Mother," she said. She spoke words in an ancient tongue.

Mapes backed toward the door.

"I know many things," Jessica went on. She studied Mapes, using her specially trained senses. "I know you came here with a knife hidden in your clothes."

"My lady . . ." Mapes held up her hands. "I brought the knife as a gift, in case you were the one our legends promised us."

"And you brought it to kill me, if I was not." Jessica waited tensely to see what Mapes would do.

Slowly Mapes reached into her dress. She brought out a knife in its sheath. She took the long, curved blade from the sheath. "Do you know this, my lady?" she asked.

Jessica tried to remember what she knew about the Fremen and their ways. "It's a crysknife."

Mapes nodded slowly. "Do you know its meaning?"

Jessica knew that somehow this was the most important question of all. She thought quickly. Knife, in the Fremen language, meant *maker of death*. "It's a maker . . .," she began.

Mapes screamed with joy and grief.

"Maker" is the key word! Jessica thought. She knew the sandworms were called Makers by the Fremen. *The knife must be a sandworm's tooth. That was close.* Out loud, she said, "Did you think that I, who know about the Great Mother, would not know the maker?"

"My lady," Mapes whispered, "we have waited for the legend to come true for so long. It is a shock when it finally happens." She began to sheathe the knife again, very slowly.

There's more to this . . . yes! Jessica thought. "Mapes, you've sheathed that blade without drawing blood."

Mapes gasped. She dropped the knife into Jessica's hands and opened her blouse. "Take the water of my life!" she cried.

Jessica took out the blade and scratched a small line on the woman's chest.

"You are ours," Mapes said, in awe. "You are the one we have waited for."

Jessica looked away from her. She knew that what Mapes said was the truth.

D URING THE NIGHT, a Harkonnen spy was discovered in the palace. He was already dead—he had committed suicide to keep from being captured. Thufir Hawat, the Duke's Mentat, was in charge of security. He decided that the palace was safe at last.

The next morning seemed much brighter. Paul went out with his father to watch the mining of spice in the desert. Gurney Halleck, the weapons master, came with them for protection. Dr. Kynes, a half-Fremen Imperial Ecologist who was an expert on Dune, was waiting for them on the landing field. He had been overseeing the change of rulers on Dune. They flew out from the palace together in an ornithopter. Paul saw fields of spice silos and huge spice-processing plants below them. Then they flew over the Shield Wall, a gigantic, cratered stretch of black rock. The Shield Wall kept the storms of the desert from burying Arrakeen Palace in sand.

As they flew, Paul asked questions about what he saw. And he realized that he seemed to know more about Dune than he had learned from his filmbooks. It was almost as if he had been born knowing about this world. He had even known exactly how to put on the water-saving Fremen stillsuits they all wore. Kynes had noticed that, too. He had been watching Paul closely all morning. "Will we see any sandworms?" Paul asked. The giant worms, which could grow to more than a thousand feet long, lived deep beneath the desert sands.

"Where there is spice and spice mining, there are always worms," Dr. Kynes answered.

"Is there a relationship between the worms and the spice?" As Paul asked the question, he saw Kynes look at him in wonder. But the ecologist only said, "The worms defend the spice sands. That's all anyone knows." Paul sensed that Kynes knew far more than he said. The man had spent his whole life studying the desert.

"There is the spice mining—that big cloud of dust." Kynes pointed. "See the spotters over it. They're watching for worms."

"I think I see a sandworm now," Duke Leto said suddenly.

"Yes!" Kynes exclaimed. He reached for the radio to call in a warning.

Paul looked out the window. He saw the sand below rippling like water with a big fish moving beneath its surface. "What happens now?" he asked.

"The carryall will come and lift off the spice harvester," Kynes answered. "Let's get closer—this will be interesting."

The ornithopter dropped down until they entered the cloud of yellow dust from the harvester. Huge waterfalls of sand spewed from the gigantic stacks on top of the machine.

A voice from the radio said, "The carryall isn't answering." Other voices repeated it.

"Harkonnen sabotage!" Duke Leto muttered. He spoke into the microphone. "This is Duke Leto Atreides. We're coming down to take you off the harvester. Get ready."

"Yes, my lord!" said the radio voice. "But we can't leave the spice . . ."

"Never mind the spice!" the Duke ordered. "Get out of there!"

The Duke's ornithopter landed by the harvester. The spotters landed their ships nearby. Paul felt the ground shaking beneath them, and heard a loud thundering noise. Men came running out of the harvester and threw themselves on board the 'thopters. The noise had grown into a terrible rumbling roar. The air sparkled with static electricity. The Duke took the controls, and his overloaded 'thopter rose heavily into the sky. Paul smelled a rich cinnamon scent from the unrefined spice on the workers' clothes.

Kynes pointed downward, yelling, "You're about to see something few people have ever seen. Watch!"

Paul looked down through the glittering air, and saw sand swirling around the harvester. Then he saw an enormous hole, twice the size of the machine, open in the sand. Spokes glistened inside it—the teeth in the mouth of a giant sandworm. Suddenly the harvester toppled over. It slid into the hole, as parts of it exploded. The sound was deafening. Paul gasped with amazement.

"What a monster!" Gurney Halleck murmured.

"Someone is going to pay for this treachery," the Duke said. "I promise."

Kynes looked over at him. Paul saw unwilling admiration in the ecologist's all-blue eyes. It was now clear to Kynes that human life was more important to the Duke than even spice.

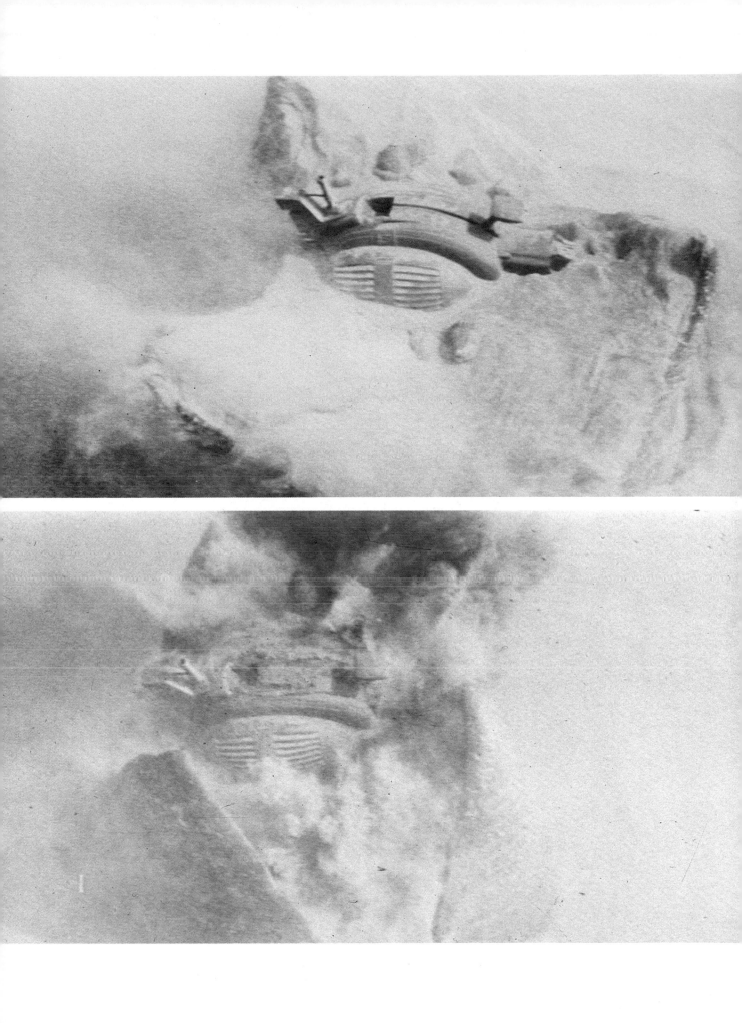

LATE THAT NIGHT Duke Leto looked in on his son's room. He saw Paul sleeping, and smiled as he turned back to the doorway again. Everyone was safe, for the moment, he thought. He did not see Paul struggle desperately to move or call out, as he left. "Father," Paul gasped. "Help me . . . I'm drugged . . ." But his father did not hear him.

The Duke walked through the endless corridors of the palace, talking to his men. He asked them about palace security and about the loyalty of the natives. He talked about spice production, but his mind was only on his family. *Jessica, my dear Jessica,* he thought. *If only we could be somewhere else, away from this terrible place, happy together.*

He walked on alone down a darkening hall. Then suddenly he heard someone whimpering with pain. He hurried forward as he saw a dark shape lying on the floor. It was the Shadout Mapes. She had been stabbed.

"What happened?" he asked. She tried to speak as he kneeled down beside her, but she died before she could answer him. As he held her body in his arms, the Duke heard the sound of the palace's shield generator begin to die down. The force field that protected the palace from attack had been sabotaged! He reached up to turn on his body shield. But before he could, a drugged dart struck him. The Duke staggered and fell to the floor.

The Duke looked up from where he lay, unable to move. He saw Dr. Yueh standing over him. At last he knew who the real traitor was—Yueh, Paul's tutor and his own trusted physician. "Why?" he gasped.

"I want to kill a man," Yueh said grimly. His face was full of bitterness and self-disgust. "Not you, my lord, but Baron Harkonnen. He is holding my wife

prisoner, to make me betray you. But I'll have my revenge on him. I'm going to put a poison tooth in your mouth. The Baron will want to get close to you, to gloat over his victory. Bite the tooth and breathe out. The poison gas will kill you both."

"I refuse," Duke Leto said.

"Do it—and in return, I'll save the lives of Paul and Jessica for you." Yueh placed the tooth in the Duke's mouth. Then he pulled the ducal signet ring from Leto's finger. "For Paul," he said.

The Duke's vision began to fade.

"When you see the Baron, remember the tooth!" Yueh hissed.

O UTSIDE THE PALACE, Harkonnen ships were landing. Their troops and the Emperor's disguised Sardaukar warriors poured into the palace. Explosions tore open the night. Smoke and flames were everywhere. The Duke's soldiers tried to fight off the unexpected attack, but they were hopelessly outnumbered. Dr. Yueh had destroyed the weirding modules that were their secret weapons. Most of them were killed; only a few escaped into the desert. The Duke and his family were taken prisoner. The House of Atreides had fallen.

Baron Harkonnen spent only a moment gloating over the bound, helpless forms of Paul and Lady Jessica. He was more interested in seeing the Duke. "We were ordered to kill them—so do it, Piter," he told his Mentat. He floated from the room.

"Take them into the desert, as the traitor Yueh told us to," Piter said to a guard. "Let the sandworms get rid of them. Their bodies must never be found." He followed the Baron out.

The guards carried Paul and his mother to an ornithopter and flew out into the desert. His mother had been gagged. She could not use The Voice, her special Bene Gesserit skill, to make the guards release them. They would be thrown out onto the dunes, to die of thirst and be eaten by sandworms.

Only he could save them now—and he had only one chance. His mother had been teaching him to use The Voice, but he had never been successful with it. This time he had to do it right. "Remove my mother's gag," he said.

One of the guards laughed. "Did you hear a noise?" he asked. The other guard shook his head.

"REMOVE HER GAG," Paul said again. And this time he felt the power of The Voice fill the words.

Slowly, slowly the guard reached out, and took the gag from Jessica's mouth.

"CUT MY SON'S BONDS," Jessica said. The guard obeyed. Paul kicked upward as his legs were freed, knocking the guard out. He leaped forward, attacking the guard at the controls. They struggled, and before Paul won the fight, the ornithopter had gone into a nosedive. It struck the jagged heights of a rock abutment in the deep desert, tearing off a wing. Desperately Paul grabbed the controls. He barely managed to bring the 'thopter down to a safe landing on the dunes below the wall.

Paul cut his mother's bonds, and they leaped out into the sand. Jessica pointed back into the ship. "I saw Dr. Yueh's sign in there. He left something under the seat. I felt it." Suddenly tears filled her eyes. "That traitor! A million deaths are not enough for Yueh!"

Paul found a box filled with survival gear under the seat. His father's signet ring lay in the box. "We have to get out of here," he told his mother. "Someone will be watching this ship." Seeing her tears, he wondered suddenly why he did not feel anything at all.

ACK IN THE BURNING Arrakeen Palace, Baron Harkonnen leaned over the helpless Duke Leto, who lay barely conscious on a stretcher. Fires and explosions lit the Baron's face with a demonic glow. He ripped the red hawk emblem from the Duke's uniform and threw it away. Then he looked up at Dr. Yueh, who was held by a Sardaukar guard. "You have done well, traitor," he said. Dr. Yueh turned his face away, filled with shame and fear. "You wish to join your wife now?" the Baron asked.

Sudden hope brightened Yueh's face. "She lives?"

The Baron smiled pityingly. "You wish to join her . . . join her, then." He waved at his Mentat Piter. Piter drew his knife, and stabbed Yueh in the back.

Yueh gasped with pain and fell forward. "You think . . ." he whispered, "that you have defeated me. You think . . . I didn't know what would happen." And he died.

"Take him away," the Baron said. He moved back to Duke Leto's side. "Where is his signet ring? It's gone." Piter shook his head.

The Duke looked up at the face of his hated enemy. He could barely think or see clearly, because he was still drugged. But he remembered what Dr. Yueh had told him, about Jessica and Paul, and about the poison tooth.

"Where is your ring?" the Baron snarled. "I must have it, to rule your lands. Where is it?"

"Come . . . closer," the Duke whispered. He knew what he must do. Tears filled his eyes. "The water . . . of my life . . . for Paul." His vision began to blur again.

The Baron frowned. "Piter! He's crying! What's he saying?" Piter moved forward, and the Baron drew back from the Duke's side.

Now, Duke Leto thought, and bit into the tooth. A rush of poison gas burst out of it. The Duke's last thoughts were of Caladan, of Jessica and Paul, of the proud Atreides flag floating on the wind. He did not know, as he died, that the wrong enemy had died with him. Only Piter was leaning over him at the fatal moment.

AT THE SAME MOMENT, far out in the desert, Paul and Jessica were running along the base of the rock abutment. Suddenly Jessica stopped in her tracks. "Leto! Leto!" she cried. She fell against the great stone wall, weeping. "He's dead! He's dead . . ."

"I know," Paul said, pulling at her arm. "Come on!" *Why don't I feel anything?* he thought. *Why?*

They ran on until they were exhausted. At last they stopped to rest in a small hollow of the Wall. Jessica sat down, weeping with grief. The sound of her weeping was lost in the rising wind. The desert sands flowed like waves on the sea. Paul stood gazing up into the night.

Two moons had risen in the night, moons he had seen once in his dreams. One of them seemed to have the shape of a mouse on its surface. As Paul stared at the moon, he had another vision. The moon seemed to explode. He saw Arrakeen Palace burning, and the face of his dead father. He saw a meteor fall into the sea by his home on Caladan. He saw an unborn child in the ocean depths, and his mother's face in the child's eyes. *The future has exploded*, he thought, amazed. *Everything has changed tonight. And I can see it. I have another kind of sight, an inner sight, now.* He knew it had come from the spice.

He opened his fist, and looked at his father's ring. "Mother," he said, "I understand it all now! The spice is in everything here—the air, the food. It changes everyone. You knew it would change me, didn't you? That's why you let us come here—so the spice could change me. With your teachings, it lets me see the future. I can see it . . . I can see it. You carry my unborn sister inside you."

Is he really the Kwisatz Haderach? Jessica thought wonderingly. *He knows.*

"You and your Bene Gesserit sisterhood!" Paul said angrily. "You try to control the future, by using everyone. But I'm *not* your Kwisatz Haderach, your tool. I'm something different, something no one expected. I'm much more. You don't even begin to know me." *I'm a seed*, he thought. He did not know what would grow from that seed; but he was afraid of it. Since he had come to Arrakis, he had felt that his life had some strange, terrible purpose, and he knew now that it was beyond his control, or anyone's. "Why did you have to let me know about the awful thing that's inside me?" he asked his mother bitterly. He felt lost and alone, and he began to tremble.

All at once he thought of his father, back on Caladan, standing above the sea. His father had told him that they must go to Dune. He had said, "New experiences help a person grow. Without change, something sleeps in us. The sleeper must awaken."

Paul took a deep breath. "Father!" he cried. "The sleeper has awakened!" He looked down, and put the Duke's ring on his finger. He was the Atreides duke, now. "Now I can cry for you, father," he whispered. His tears fell at last.

After they had rested a while longer, Paul and Jessica started out across the desert. They knew that their only hope was to find a group of Fremen. The desert people might take them in, and hide them from the Harkonnens.

But first they had to cross the sea of dunes that lay ahead of them. Sand-worms lived beneath the sand, and would sense their footsteps. But they had no other choice.

They planted the thumper that was in their survival kit. It was a machine made to lure sandworms away from desert travelers. "We have to move fast," Paul told his mother. "A worm will come soon. Remember to walk without rhythm so that it won't come after us instead of the thumper."

Jessica nodded, and they began to walk unevenly over the dunes. Lightning lit the sky, and they saw the rocky ground they must reach far ahead. They heard the thumper start behind them. They kept walking, until their legs began to ache, but the rocks seemed to get no closer. The slippery sand flowed like water under their feet. They began to feel as if they had been walking forever.

Then, suddenly, they heard a worm coming. A hissing thunder began to shake the sand. The thumper stopped behind them—the worm had swallowed it.

"Hurry!" Paul shouted. He looked back, and saw the worm start after them. A huge mound of sand swept toward them like a tidal wave. "Run!" he screamed.

"I can't!" Jessica cried. She looked back, and saw the worm coming. She ran.

All at once their feet found solid ground. They scrambled up into a narrow gap in the rocky cliff, just as the worm's head rose out of the sand. All they could see was its mouth—an eighty-foot circle of knifelike teeth and blackness. The worm began to bang mindlessly at the rock around them. They climbed higher into the narrow cleft as the wall began to crumble. The worm swallowed huge chunks of stone below them. Its stomach was a roaring furnace that could digest anything. Its breath was like a hurricane, and smelled of cinnamon.

"Cinnamon . . . the spice! Do you smell it?" Paul gasped to his mother. She nodded. Paul felt another vision fill his mind as he smelled the spice. It showed him the truth about why the worms and the spice were always found together. *I know Dune's secret*, Paul thought. *The worm makes the spice . . . the spice makes the worm*. The spice and the sandworms were the same alien creature, in different stages of its life. They were part of a great natural cycle on Dune.

The worm struck the rock again, breaking away half the wall. Paul fell from his hiding place and tumbled down and down the slope. At last he landed in the sand. Frantically he scrambled back up the cliff to another ledge. He was barely out of reach.

But just as the worm rose up for its final attack, he heard a distant thumping begin. The sandworm turned away as if it was under a spell, and disappeared into the sand. *Another thumper*, Paul thought, dazed. He climbed back to where his mother stood.

"Are you all right?" he asked breathlessly.

"Yes." Jessica nodded. Tears of relief ran down her cheeks. "What happened? Why did it leave?"

"Someone started another thumper. We're not alone."

"Look." Jessica pointed. "There are steps cut in the rock here."

"Yes," Paul whispered. They began to climb up the dark, narrow crack in the wall.

As they reached the top of the cliff, a sudden flash of lightning lit up the night. They saw a band of Fremen waiting silently up ahead.

"These may be the ones Shadout Mapes told us of," one of the Fremen said. "Are you trained in the ways of the desert?" he asked Jessica.

"No," she said calmly, "but I have other useful training."

The Fremen leader studied Jessica and Paul for a long moment. "I will keep the boy," he said at last. "But the water-fat woman cannot live in the desert." He began to draw his knife. All at once Jessica turned, moving too quickly to follow, and froze the Fremen leader with The Voice. She held him by the throat and

took his knife. At the same time, Paul ran up the rocky slope, looking down on the rest of the Fremen. They began to fire darts at him.

"Stop!" their leader shouted. "She'll break my neck. She has the weirding way! Why didn't you tell us?" he gasped. "If you can do that, you're worth ten times your weight in water. Teach us how to do it, and you will both have sanctuary with us."

"We will teach you. You have my word as a Bene Gesserit," Jessica said. She let him go.

"It is the legend," one of the Fremen whispered.

"Do you think my son is your Promised One?" Jessica asked. She knew that Fremen legends said an offworlder would come to lead the natives against their oppressors.

"The legend needs testing," the Fremen leader answered. He picked up his knife. "But we must go now. Your son has much to learn."

"We have much to teach each other," Jessica said.

Up on the hill, Paul suddenly found someone standing behind him—a girl. She was very thin, and her dark hair was pulled up in a tight knot on top of her head. But as she looked at him, the beauty of her spirit filled her eyes. Paul realized that she was the same girl he had seen in his visions. *So beautiful*, he thought.

"I am Chani," she said, "daughter of Dr. Kynes. I would not have let you harm my people."

Paul remembered Dr. Kynes, the half-Fremen ecologist who had shown him the spice mining. He followed Chani down the hill.

"I am called Stilgar," the Fremen leader said to Paul and Jessica. He studied Paul again. "I sense you have great strength in you. You shall be known as Usul, which means *strength*. That is your secret name. But you must choose a name which we can call you openly."

Paul thought a moment. "What do you call the little mouse that hops—the one whose shape is on the moon?"

The Fremen laughed. "We call it Muad'Dib."

"I don't want to give up the name my father gave me," Paul said. "Could I be called Paul Muad'Dib?"

"You are Paul Muad'Dib." Stilgar nodded. "And your mother will be a Sayyadina, a wise woman, among us. We welcome you." The Fremen led them away into the night.

They walked for many hours. The night's Mouse Moon set. Dawn came, and the huge, blazing sun rose into the sky. All day Paul and Jessica wearily followed the Fremen through the desert. At last, at dusk, Chani led Paul to the top of a sand dune. They stared at the many-colored sunset. In the distance, Paul heard strange noises echoing. A huge band of rock rose from the desert up ahead. "Sietch Tabr," Chani said, pointing. "That is where we live."

The Fremen band entered Sietch Tabr, their hidden underground fortress, through a secret opening in the rock. Smooth, dark passages and steps led away, downward, in all directions. A moaning wind filled the empty halls. The Fremen had many huge hidden wind traps. They used the strong desert winds as an energy supply.

Stilgar led Paul and Jessica down one passageway after another. The wind sound grew louder. The air grew colder and damper. Jessica and Paul glanced at each other. Neither of them quite dared to ask the questions in their minds. At last they reached a place that made Paul stare in wonder. It was a huge underground lake, lying black and silent in the darkness. *I've seen this place in a dream,* Paul thought. He looked at Chani. All the Fremen were staring at the water, as if it were a holy thing.

"A treasure," Paul said.

"More than a treasure," Stilgar answered. "We have thousands of these places. When we have enough, we will change the face of Arrakis, our world. We will make the desert bloom. Listen!" They all listened to the drip of water falling. "The rocks of Dune hold many secrets," he said.

Chani's hand touched Paul's shoulder. He turned, looking into her eyes. "Tell me of your homeworld, Usul," she whispered.

Paul remembered his dream of this place and of Chani. Emotion filled him until he could not speak. He touched her face gently with his hand. They stood together listening to the water for a moment. Then she moved away again.

Another group of Fremen came down the hallway. They spoke to Chani as Paul watched. He saw her face fill with shock and loss. She did not cry; the Fremen almost never cried, because it wasted water. But he could tell that something terrible had happened. "What is it?" he asked Stilgar.

"Chani's father is dead," Stilgar said. "The Harkonnens killed him."

"Both of us have lost our fathers, because of the Harkonnens," Paul said. He felt the strange bond between Chani and himself grow even stronger. He wanted to go to her and comfort her, but the other Fremen led her away up the hall.

AFTER HIS TREACHEROUS VICTORY, Baron Harkonnen returned home to his grim world, Giedi Prime. He took a special prisoner with him from Dune. A few days later, the Baron went with his evil nephew, Feyd, to visit their prisoner in the dungeons. The prisoner was Thufir Hawat, Duke Leto's Mentat. They had captured him on Dune. The Baron had kept him alive for his own evil reasons.

"Feyd," the Baron said, "I've given Thufir Hawat a horrible poison. He knows it. He is afraid to die in such terrible agony. Every day I will give him the antidote to the poison, as long as he serves me faithfully. Duke Leto killed my Mentat Piter. Now I have his Thufir instead. He is one of the finest Mentats in the universe . . . and he's mine, Feyd . . . all mine." The Baron chuckled and rubbed his swollen hands together.

DAYS AND WEEKS PASSED, back on Dune, as Paul and Jessica began to learn the ways of the Fremen. Paul quickly found that the Fremen were not primitive nomads at all. They had secret gardens in the desert, windmills for power, and advanced machinery hidden in their sietches.

Dr. Yueh had hidden the plans for Duke Leto's weirding module with the survival equipment he left for Paul and Jessica. The Fremen were able to build more of the weapons, using the plans. Then Paul called the Fremen of Sietch Tabr together. He knew their secret knowledge would make it much easier for him to teach them to use the weirding modules.

Thousands of Fremen gathered in the Hall of Rites. Paul stood on a rock ledge among a crowd of Fremen monks. A giant wind organ moaned eerie music.

"We think you may be the 'voice from the outer world' our teachings promised would come," one monk said. "You must pass tests before we are sure . . . you must conquer the beast of the desert, the sandworm, first. But tell us now of the power you have brought us from the outer world. It can help us defeat our offworlder enemies."

I am only a seed, Paul said to himself. He gathered his courage, and turned to speak to the crowd. "I am Usul . . . Paul Muad'Dib."

"Muad'Dib," the crowd murmured.

No one ever dreamed there were so many Fremen, Paul thought. Out loud, he said, "Our shared enemy, the Harkonnens, rule Dune again. Stilgar, your leader, has asked me and my mother to get rid of the Harkonnens. We must do more than that. We must try to destroy all the spice mining on Dune. The Spacing Guild and the entire universe depend on spice. There is a saying that 'he who can destroy a thing, controls that thing.' Unless we control the spice, we will never win against the Empire."

Paul looked out over the crowd. "I will take one hundred of your warriors and train them to use the weirding module. Those one hundred will train the thousands that are left. We will attack the Harkonnen spice miners. When the supply of spice stops, then the Baron and even the Emperor will have to deal with us. Dune will become the center of the universe." *So this is why I have come here*, Paul thought.

Paul chose one hundred Fremen and led them to a training area. Jessica and Stilgar sat watching as he began to teach them. Paul stood beside a large pillar of rock. Nearby, a drummer beat out a loud, echoing rhythm. Another large block of stone was being moved back and forth over coarse sand. The sound it made added to the powerful rhythm.

Paul said, "The weirding way has been a Bene Gesserit secret for a long time. With my mother's help, my father found a way to imitate some of its effects with this weapon. You can be the best fighters in the universe when you know the weirding way." He looked from face to face. "You know about sound and motion. They are the keys to this weapon. I will teach you how those things can build and heal, or destroy."

He moved to the large pillar of rock as he spoke. "Orato!" He called one of the Fremen up to the rock. "Kick it," he ordered, and the man did. "Hit it. Yell at it." The man did those things too, but nothing happened to the stone. The other Fremen laughed.

"Move back!" Paul ordered them. He moved away from the rock. He switched on the weirding module he wore. He made a small sound, which the weirding module made much louder. "Chuksa!" Paul shouted. The stone shattered into pieces. The Fremen shouted their amazement.

"This is *part* of what I will teach you," Paul told them, "and much more. Through sound and motion you will be able to paralyze nerves, shatter bones, set fires, or suffocate your enemies. We will fight until no Harkonnens are left to breathe the air of Dune." And he thought grimly, *To avenge my father, I will turn you into killing machines.* The Fremen had been waiting for the Prophet their legends told them would come. They were ready to begin a holy war against the Harkonnens, and even the Emperor himself. There were millions of Fremen in hidden sietches all over Arrakis—a vast army that no offworlders knew about. They were ready to take back their world.

The Fremen believed that Paul might be the leader they had waited for—and Paul knew now they were right. This was his terrible purpose. He believed that he could lead them to victory. But he knew the battle would cause great suffering. Many good people would die. He wished again that he had never had to face the destiny to which he had been born.

Jessica sat sadly watching her son train the Fremen. She knew what he must be feeling now. But she knew he had no choice. Stilgar turned to her. "Sayyadina," he said. "Our Reverend Mother is very old. She believes you have come to take her place. It is time for you to take the Water of Life, and become our new Reverend Mother." Long ago the Fremen had made some of the Bene Gesserit missionary teachings into part of their own religion. They used the Water of Life to look into the future, and called their holy leader a Reverend Mother, as the Bene Gesserit did.

Jessica did not answer for a moment. She knew that the Water of Life, the Truthsayer drug, was very dangerous. It could harm her unborn child, or even kill her. But she knew that she could not refuse. If she did, she and Paul might lose the Fremen's belief in them. She, too, had no choice. It was her destiny, as well. "I will try," she said.

"Then we will prepare for the rite," Stilgar said.

Later that day Paul and Jessica entered the huge Hall of Rites. Thousands of Fremen were gathering there again to watch the ritual. Paul saw Chani across the hall. He could barely take his eyes from her face. The Reverend Mother Ramallo, a frail but beautiful old woman, was carried into the hall on a litter. She gave Paul and his mother a long, strange look. Horns sounded, voices sang. Incense burners filled the air with the smell of spice. Jessica was led to a throne beside the Reverend Mother.

Through an opening in a stone wall, Paul could see a large sealed chamber with a thirty-foot baby sandworm inside it. Suddenly water began to fill the chamber. The worm writhed and leaped violently. Then, as Paul watched in horror, the worm began to turn inside out. It died, and the water turned a deep blue. Fremen began to fill sacks with the blue liquid.

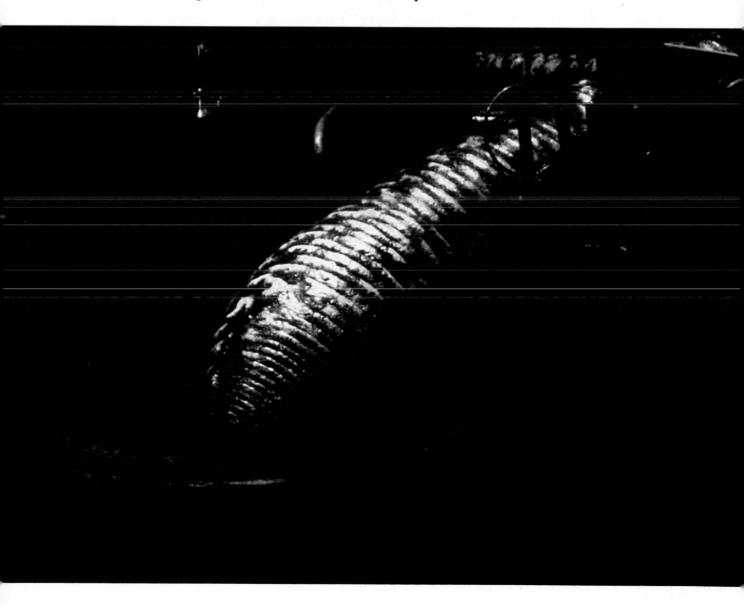

"That is the Water of Life," Stilgar whispered to Paul. "It holds the secrets of the universe."

Paul only knew that it was a deadly poison, and that his mother was about to drink it. He remembered the Reverend Mother Mohiam, back on Caladan, saying that no man had ever drunk it and lived. He watched his mother with his heart beating too fast.

Fremen monks carried the sacks of water to Jessica's throne. "Here is the Water of Life," one monk said. "Let it judge if you are a Reverend Mother! Drink it, and pass within!"

Jessica took the sack. She knew that she must change the poisonous Water of Life inside her with her own willpower. It would let her see the future if she could, and kill her if she could not. She swallowed a mouthful of the water. Her body began to shake with convulsions. Wild, terrifying hallucinations began to fill her mind. She screamed, and the Reverend Mother Ramallo screamed with her.

Jessica felt as if she were drowning in a pool of blue water. She fought with all her strength to save herself. She used her secret Bene Gesserit powers to turn the poison in her body into something new. Suddenly the pool of blue water turned pure and crystal clear. She was not drowning anymore. She was floating, in a place outside of time. She had changed the Water of Life.

She felt the Reverend Mother Ramallo's mind enter her own. The Reverend Mother's thoughts spoke to her, in a way that only the Bene Gesserit had ever done. "I have waited a long time for you," the Reverend Mother said. "Here is my life." All of her knowledge, and all of the knowledge of every Reverend Mother before her, filled Jessica's mind—and the mind of her unborn child. At the end of all the memories was the black, terrifying place no one had ever looked into. Sparks were blown about in a roaring darkness. There was a strange shape moving in the darkness—a Third-Stage Navigator. *What is this?* Jessica thought. *Is this what kills the men who enter here?* Jessica pulled herself, and her child, away from the whirlpool of darkness. She soothed her child's terror. Then she let her mind rise into the light of day again. *We will both be Reverend Mothers,* Jessica thought to her child.

She opened her eyes. She saw the old Reverend Mother slumped forward, dead, beside her. Fremen monks came and carried her body gently away. Another monk held the sack before Jessica again.

"Change it, so that we may all drink it," he said. Jessica opened her mouth, and blue water poured out of it into the sack. The monk swirled the bag, and sipped from it. "It is changed!" he called.

She did it, Paul thought, weak with relief.

All the Fremen turned to look at him. "It is the prophecy!" they murmured. Their legends said that the mother of their offworld Prophet would be a holy woman. They began to chant, "Muad'Dib, Muad'Dib . . ." Their chanting filled the hall. Paul knew they would do anything for his mother or for him now.

A monk brought the bag of water to Paul. "Drink it. It's safe. Our Reverend Mother has changed it."

Paul drank. But he knew that in order to be a true prophet he must drink the unchanged Water of Life, like his mother, and see what it showed him. As the monk moved away, Paul saw Chani drinking. His vision began to grow bright and dark from the Water. Chani turned to face him. She came to his side.

"Come with me," she whispered. She led him from the Hall, down a dark passageway. They held each other, and kissed.

"Chani, I love you," Paul said. "I've always loved you." They kissed again. He felt giddy and strange, filled with happiness and fear all at once. He seemed to see the future stretching out before him. He saw brief moments of peace and happiness with Chani, among years of war and strife. In the distance he could still hear the Fremen chanting his name, like the roar of an ocean.

TIME PASSED LIKE WATER dripping into the sietch's hidden lake. Weeks turned into months for Paul and his mother, safe in Sietch Tabr. Paul's love for Chani grew. His eyes turned completely blue, like the natives' eyes, from the use of spice. In time his sister was born, and his mother named her Alia. Alia could speak from the moment she was born. She was born knowing everything her mother knew.

Paul continued to train the Fremen and to learn their ways. They became experts with the weirding module. They shouted his name, "Muad'Dib!" and walls crumbled. *My own name is a killing word now,* Paul thought grimly. *Will it be a healing word, as well?*

Stilgar chose fifteen of the fiercest Fremen fighters to be Paul's own guard— the Fedaykin. They wore a blood-red mark on their sleeves. Paul led his warriors

on raids against the Harkonnens' spice mines. Rabban, the Baron's second sadistic nephew, ruled Dune for his uncle. But no matter how cruelly he tried to fight back, he could not stop the Fremen. *If only you could see them, Father,* Paul thought proudly.

Paul had become a Fremen in every way but one—he had never ridden a sandworm. Riding a sandworm was a test of courage and skill every Fremen had to pass. Paul knew he must pass it too, in order to really be their leader. Stilgar taught him how it was done. At last Paul went out into the desert with Stilgar and the Fedaykin. They set out a thumper, and waited for a sandworm.

Paul stood on a dune. He heard the thunder of a worm approaching. It was a large worm, traveling deep beneath the sand. He held two hooks, and tried to remember what Stilgar had taught him. He must use the hooks to pry loose a plate of the hard shell that protected the worm from the sand. He must not get too close, or he would be buried in flying sand, or eaten alive.

The tidal wave of sand that showed the worm was coming swept toward him at terrifying speed. He stood frozen, holding his breath, as the sandworm roared closer. The noise grew deafening. At last the worm burst from the wave of sand. Lightning sparked around it. It was huge—much bigger than he had imagined. Its head towered a hundred and twenty-five feet in the air. Waves of heat poured from its open mouth, where a thousand teeth glistened.

Paul ran through the sand beside the worm. He planted a hook under a ten-foot-wide piece of its shell. The worm almost dragged him down into the choking sand, but he stayed on his feet. He pried the shell loose. The sand scraped the worm's tender skin.

Suddenly the worm rolled over, to escape the sand. Paul was lifted higher and higher into the air. He climbed up the worm's gigantic body. He planted both his hooks in its tender breathing holes. Now the worm was under his control. *I'm a sandrider at last!* he thought triumphantly.

He made the worm slow down and turn back to where the others waited. They used their own hooks to climb up onto the worm. "Long live the fighters!" he cried. The Fremen returned the traditional shout. Together they rode on across the desert.

MONTHS PASSED, and then years. Paul continued to lead the Fremen in their sneak attacks against the Harkonnen's spice supply. And in time, the Baron's nephew Rabban could no longer disguise the losses. He had thought he was very lucky to be put in charge of Dune by his uncle. But that was before the mysterious Muad'Dib and his desert raiders had appeared. They had destroyed most of his spice mining with their endless guerilla warfare.

Now Rabban was having a screaming fit in the Great Hall of Arrakeen Palace. "Falsify the reports about the spice," he shouted. "We can't hide all our losses, but don't tell my uncle we've lost two hundred harvesters and forty carryalls! Don't tell him about the spice silos that were destroyed!" He thrashed furiously in the black steel tub where he sat. "I will catch this Muad'Dib and suck the blood from him! *Suck the blood from him!*" he screamed.

MEANWHILE, far out in the desert, Paul Muad'Dib was leading his men on another successful raid. Smoke billowed from a burning spice harvester as he stood on a dune looking down at the battlefield. This time, his raiders had accidentally surprised a band of smugglers as they attacked the spice miners.

Looking over their captives, Paul suddenly saw a familiar face. "Gurney Halleck!" he shouted. He could hardly believe his eyes. It was his old teacher, his father's weapons master. Gurney had escaped the Harkonnens' attack on Arrakeen Palace. He had joined the smugglers in the desert to keep fighting them. He had believed that the whole Atreides family, whom he had served for so long, had been murdered.

"You know me?" Gurney asked in disbelief. At first he did not recognize Paul, who looked like a Fremen. But then he saw the Duke's signet ring on Paul's hand, and his face changed. "Paul? Is it really Paul?" His eyes filled with tears, and he hugged his former student. "They said you were dead. . . . You young pup! You young pup!" he cried joyfully.

"Come with me to Sietch Tabr," Paul said. "My mother will be so glad to see you."

BACK IN SIETCH TABR, Paul's baby sister Alia was fighting another kind of battle. A girl named Subiay stood in the sietch hallway calling her names. Ever since she had been born, the other children had tormented her because she acted different. She *was* different—she had been born knowing everything her mother knew. Her mind was the mind of an adult, trapped in the body of a child. She knew why the others called her a demon. She knew she wasn't a demon, but she was lonely and frustrated just the same. She had no friends. Only her mother and Paul, and Harah, her nurse, really loved her. And even they didn't understand her problems.

"You don't understand anything, Subiay," she said to the other child. "I have a right to use my mind. I have a right to use my eyes, and my hands —" She moved closer to the other child. "And my voice!" She used The Voice. The other girl screamed with pain and ran off down the hall. Alia stood silently, all alone again.

AND FAR ACROSS THE GALAXY, the Emperor stood alone in his golden room again. He was facing another visit from the Guild. This time only a First-Stage Navigator had come to the palace. A First-Stage Navigator still looked human, although he wore a tank suit filled with spice gas. But his words were just as threatening as the last message from the Guild. "Emperor Shaddam IV, you have one last chance to control the situation on Dune."

"What do you mean, one last—" the Emperor began.

"Do not speak! Listen!" the Guildsman ordered. "You have failed to kill Paul Atreides. He is in the desert with the Fremen. The spice is in great danger. You must stop him, or all is lost." The Guildsmen had used the spice to look into the future. They did not like what they saw. "Correct the situation or you will live out your life in a pain amplifier. I order you to send fifty legions of Sardaukar troops to Dune."

"Fifty legions?" The Emperor was shocked. "That's all our reserves. Do you want to destroy all life on Dune?" But he knew the answer must be yes. Suddenly the Emperor felt as if he was not the Emperor of anything, anymore. The Guild was controlling his Empire, and him.

The Guildsman left his chambers without another word.

"Who is this Paul Atreides to the Guild?" he whispered. "And why?"

THE EMPEROR SENT OUT ORDERS, obeying the Guild's commands. His own commands were obeyed as quickly, and soon the sky above Dune began to fill with spaceships. The final battle was about to begin.

In Sietch Tabr, Paul woke out of a nightmare about sandworms attacking. Blinking in the darkness, he looked up into Chani's face.

"You were calling my name," she said softly. "It frightened me."

Paul remembered a vision of Chani looking down at him. It was the last vision he had had in a long time, and now it had come true. He knew that he could no longer see the future—unless he drank the Water of Life. He knew it might kill him. But it was his destiny, and now he had to face it. "Chani, I *have* to drink the Water of Life."

"No! Paul, please," she said. "I've seen men who have tried. I've seen how they die." She shuddered.

"I am dead to everyone, unless I become what I . . . may . . . be." He shook his head. "Only the Water of Life can free what can save us." If he was going to be the prophet everyone thought he was, then he would learn it now. And if he was not, he knew that he must find that out before he led his people to defeat instead of victory. He remembered his father saying to him, *"The sleeper must awaken."*

"I must drink the sacred water," he said. "You have to help me, Chani. All the paths to the future that I could see before are hidden from me in darkness. We have to go now."

Paul and Chani and the Fedaykin left the sietch. They walked silently out into the sparkling desert night. In the hollow of a huge dune, Paul stopped and turned to Chani. They looked into each other's eyes for a long moment. Then Paul nodded to the Fedaykin. They tied him up quickly with ropes. Then they stood back again, waiting quietly. Their legends had told him this would happen. Chani held the blue Water of Life out to Paul.

"Hurry!" Paul whispered tensely. "All I see is darkness."

"Paul, I will love you forever, in life or death," Chani said. "You are my life." She poured the blue water into Paul's mouth.

As Paul drank, he wondered, *What is it that waits for me in this darkness?* Suddenly he screamed and fell to his knees, as the poison struck him. The desert disappeared into a deeper darkness.

Back in her chambers in the sietch Jessica woke in the night. Alia woke beside her. Their minds were filled with pain. "What's wrong?" Jessica gasped.

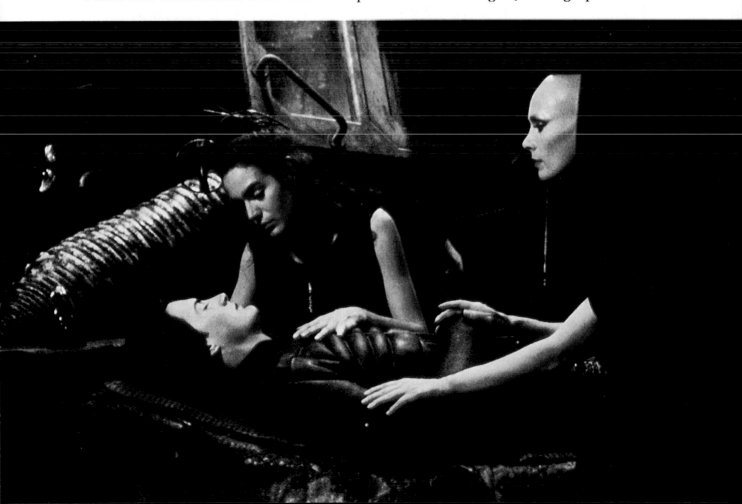

"It's Paul," Alia cried. "He's taken the Water of Life."

They clung to each other in the night. They felt Paul's pain. They knew that their own lives were part of his great destiny. The plans of many generations of the Bene Gesserit and the Spacing Guild had collided at last. Paul was caught at their center. Only he could save Dune—but first he had to save himself.

On another plane of space and time, where only the mind could go, Paul's mind met the mind of a Third-Stage Navigator. The Navigator's mind was as twisted by his lust for power as his body was deformed. He wanted the Guild to rule the universe. He knew that only Paul could stop them. He tried to destroy Paul's mind. Paul's body writhed with pain, back in the desert, as his mind fought the Navigator's. He cried out, and a great wind rose in the desert. In the other world, the sound became a powerful weapon, as Paul used the weirding way. The sound destroyed the Navigator. Paul was free. He could see into the future, and see his destiny clearly at last. He saw the secret behind everything, and the key to saving Dune.

In the desert, the roar of an approaching worm filled the night. Chani and the Fedaykin, standing guard over Paul's body, looked up in horror. Seven giant worms were coming toward them at once. The worms broke through the sand and rose up, towering over them. The worms hovered, waiting.

Chani looked at the Fedaykin, and then at Paul's body, which lay as still as death. With trembling hands, she cut the ropes that held him. The whole desert seemed to tremble.

Paul's eyes opened. He sat up slowly.

Chani stared at him in awe. "Paul . . . Paul . . ." was all she could say.

Paul saw his father's image, like a ghost, in his mind. He got to his feet. "Father! Father!" he shouted. "The sleeper *has* awakened!" The words echoed across the desert. The worms bent back into the sand and thundered away.

At last Chani asked, "Paul, have you seen the future?"

He shook his head. "I've seen the *now*. The time of the final battle has come. The space above Dune is filled with Guild ships. The Emperor is there, and the Baron, and all the Great Houses. The Guild thinks they have us trapped. But now I know a secret they don't. Now I know how to cause a chain reaction that will destroy all spice . . . forever."

"You can't," Chani gasped.

"I can," he said. "I understand how the spice and the sandworms are related. The sandworms grow from the spice, and cause more spice to form. They are the Makers, as the Fremen say. They are part of an endless circle. And I can destroy the circle with the water from the sietches. It can destroy the spice, and become the Water of Death. How the Guild trembles when they think of me!" He looked back toward the sietch. "We will let all the Fremen know I've drunk the Water of Life. Now they will truly believe I am the leader their legends told of. The time has come to call them all together and attack." *Father*, he thought, *our time has come.*

T HE FREMEN OF THE SIETCH spread the word that Paul was their long-awaited Prophet. Other Fremen began to gather from all over the planet, by thousands, and then millions. They chanted the name of Muad'Dib. They prepared for a war against the evil tyrants who had made their world suffer. They waited for Paul to lead them against the Emperor's coming attack. "Long live the fighters!" they cried.

S EVERAL DAYS LATER, Paul, his old teacher Gurney Halleck, and Stilgar watched from the Shield Wall as the Emperor's forces landed at Arrakeen. A gigantic steel tent opened below the Emperor's own ship. It was his palace and his protection.

Paul looked up at the sky. "A sandstorm is rising of a magnitude and intensity never before seen anywhere in the universe, just as we planned," he said. "Gurney, when it hits, I want you to blast an opening in the Shield Wall. Stilgar, do you see a sign of worms coming this way?"

The others laughed. "More worms than even God has seen," Stilgar said. "We planted thousands of thumpers."

Paul looked out at the desert. He saw it rippling like an ocean as the worms came. A vast army of Fremen waited below to catch and ride them. He smiled. "Everything is ready," he said.

IN THE SKY OVER ARRAKEEN PALACE, a thousand Harkonnen ships screamed down to a landing. Baron Harkonnen had been ordered to see the Emperor. He entered the huge steel tent where the Emperor sat waiting with his advisor, the Reverend Mother Mohiam, beside him. "Why have you brought me here?" the Emperor asked the Baron. "You know I hate to travel."

The bloated Baron cringed. "Your Highness, there must be some mistake. I didn't call you here."

"Your failure did," the Emperor said coldly. "Your harsh rule of this world has driven the people to rebellion." *And even worse, you didn't kill Paul Atreides,* he thought. *You made the Guild angry at me.* "You forced me to come here to set things straight . . . personally. Bring in the messenger!" he ordered

A tiny girl dressed all in black was brought into the room by guards. It was Alia. She said, "I am the messenger from Muad'Dib. Poor Emperor, I'm afraid my brother won't be very pleased with you."

The Reverend Mother Mohiam stared at the little girl. Suddenly she gasped and clutched her throat. "Kill this child! Kill her!" she shrieked. She pointed at Alia, who smiled at her. "Get out of my mind!"

"Not until you tell them who my brother *really* is," Alia said.

"Paul Muad'Dib," the Reverend Mother gasped. "Duke Paul Atreides."

Baron Harkonnen's mouth fell open. The Emperor turned pale, as he looked at the Guildsmen standing across the room. Alia smiled happily.

Outside the wind rose. A sandstorm raged beyond the Shield Wall. "Alia is keeping up with the storm," Paul said to Gurney and Stilgar. Gurney gave the order, and huge explosions blasted the hole in the Wall. Blinding sand raged through it toward Arrakeen. Paul's warriors followed. The attack had begun.

Everyone in the Emperor's tent heard the explosions. "My brother is coming with many Fremen warriors," Alia said.

Just then, a Sardaukar soldier rushed into the tent. "The Shield Wall is gone!" he said.

"Impossible!" the Emperor exclaimed.

"Not for my brother," Alia said. "He is here now."

"Baron," the Emperor ordered, "throw this little monster out into the storm."

Alia shrank down, looking frightened. Baron Harkonnen grabbed her with his heavy hands. But suddenly she turned and struck at his face. He cried out. Alia held out the poisoned needle she had hidden in her hand. "Meet the Atreides gom jabbar!" she cried.

The Baron sputtered and died. His suspensors held him up in the air, a ghastly corpse.

Suddenly a wall of the Emperor's palace tent exploded. "Into your ship, Your Majesty!" a guard shouted. Alia escaped as they ran to the ship's elevator.

Out in the desert, Paul smiled grimly. He could read his sister's mind. He knew their father had been avenged. He began the final attack.

The battle and the storm raged around Arrakeen Palace. Countless sandworms poured through the broken Shield Wall, terrifying even the bravest of the Sardaukar officers. Each sandworm was ridden by hundreds of armed Fremen. Even the Sardaukar with their energy weapons were no match for them. The worms swallowed the Emperor's troops by the thousands. The Fremen warriors killed the few that were left. Any Imperial ships that were still in the air crashed in the blinding storm.

More than a thousand Fremen warriors battled their way through to the last line of the Emperor's defenses. The troop of Sardaukar warriors surrounding the Emperor's palace tent were overpowered by the Fremen. Finally, the Emperor himself was captured. Paul and the Fremen were victorious.

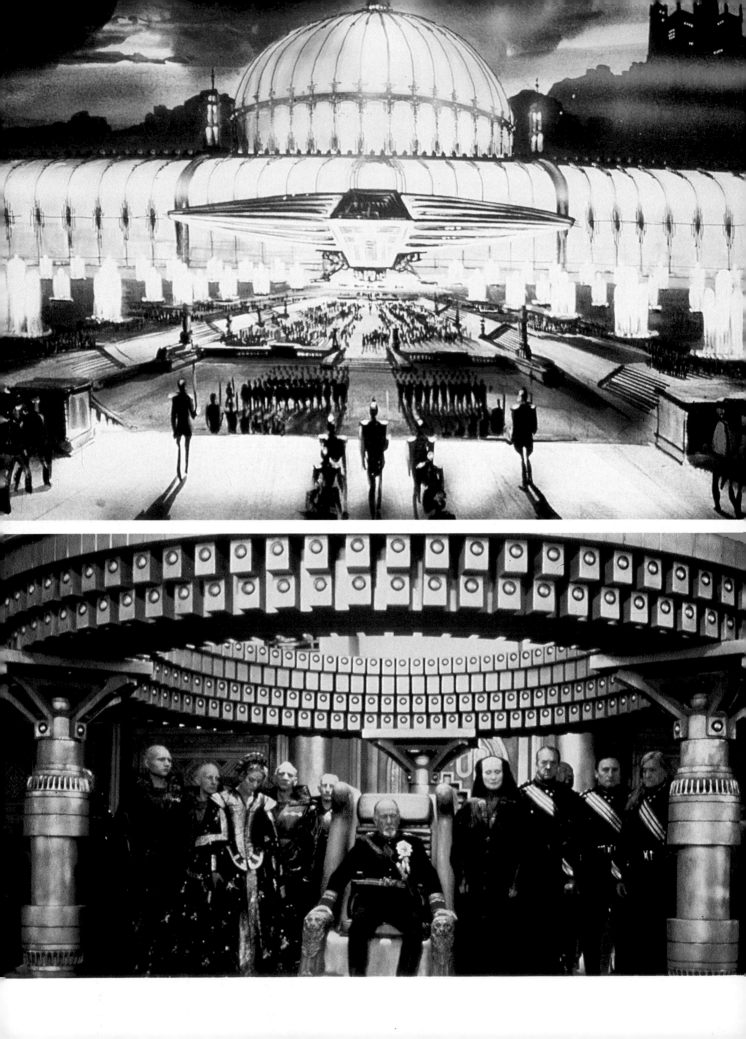

THE NEXT DAY, Paul entered Arrakeen Palace. He was dusty and tired and still wearing his battered stillsuit. The new desert wind moaned through the palace halls like the voices of ghosts. Painful memories filled Paul as he looked around. But so much had happened to him since he had last been in the palace; so much time had passed. He felt very old. The memories almost seemed to belong to someone else, now. He could never go back to what he had been once. He put his arm around Chani and looked at his mother.

Jessica stood with Alia at her side. Both mother and daughter wore the black robes of a Bene Gesserit Reverend Mother. Jessica's eyes were filled with sorrow. "What are you going to do now?" she asked.

"Watch," Paul said. Gurney and several guards led in the Emperor. His daughter, Princess Irulan, and his advisor, the Reverend Mother Mohiam, were with him. There were also several generals and Guildsmen, Baron Harkonnen's nephew Feyd, and Thufir Hawat. Baron Harkonnen was dead and eaten by sandworms, and so was his other nephew, Rabban. Many Fremen stood around the room as guards. Paul looked at one face after another. Feyd smiled evilly. The Emperor glared. Paul looked at Princess Irulan, and she looked away.

"Gurney," Paul said. "I see Thufir Hawat, my father's Mentat, among the captives. Let him go."

Gurney nodded sadly. He waved to Thufir, who stepped forward to face Paul. Thufir looked very old and bewildered. It hurt Paul to see what the Harkonnens had done to his former teacher. But he also noticed a strange, tense look fill the Emperor's face as he watched Thufir. Paul used his mental skills to find out why.

Thufir has a knife, Paul thought. *The Emperor thinks he will use it to kill me.* Aloud, he said, "You have served my family for three generations, Thufir. You may ask me now for anything you want. Anything at all." And he added quietly, "Do you need my life, Thufir?" He turned away, with his back to Thufir. "My life is yours," he said.

Thufir's eyes grew wide and sad.

"I mean this, Thufir," Paul said. "If you're going to strike, do it now."

Thufir raised his hand. Jessica gasped. But the old Mentat held the knife out to the Emperor. "Did you think for one moment that I would fail my Duke twice?" he asked. And he killed himself, instead.

Paul kneeled down by his teacher. "Carry this noble Atreides warrior away," he said softly, to his Fremen. "Do him all honor."

More Guildsmen entered the room. Seeing them, Paul said, "Emperor Shaddam IV, there is a Guild Heighliner up above us, holding all the Great Houses of the Empire. Send them home."

"How dare you speak to me—" the Emperor began.

"Stop your speaking!" a Guildsman ordered.

Paul looked at the Guildsman. "You are afraid of what I can do. I will show the one hiding deep in the ship up there what I can *really* do." Paul reached out with his mind. He found the mind of the Third-Stage Navigator, in the spice gas–filled control room of the spaceship far above them. *I have the power to destroy the spice forever*, he thought. *You know I do.*

The Navigator gave a terrible moan. The Guildsmen down in the palace also began to moan and scream. They ran for the doorways, but the Fremen stopped them. Paul knew that the Guild would have to obey him now.

The Reverend Mother glared at Paul. "Don't try to use your powers on me!" Paul said angrily. "Try looking into that place where you're afraid to look. You'll find me there, staring back at you! You Bene Gesserit are as bad as the Guild. For ninety generations you've worked secretly to produce the one person you needed to rule the galaxy. Here I stand. But I'll never belong to you."

"Stop him, Jessica!" The Reverend Mother ordered.

"Stop him yourself," Jessica answered evenly.

"You partly understood what human beings needed, to become a better people, *in the beginning,*" Paul told the Reverend Mother. "But in time you forgot your noble goals. You tried to control human breeding and create a great leader. But it was for your own selfish reasons, not to help humanity. How little you really understand."

"You mustn't speak of—" the Reverend Mother began.

"SILENCE!" Paul shouted, using The Voice. The Reverend Mother was thrown against a wall by the power of his shout. "I remember your gom jabbar, now you remember mine," Paul said. "I can kill with a word."

One of the Fedaykin quoted a Fremen prophecy: "His word shall carry death to those who stand against the righteous."

"The righteous!" Feyd, Baron Harkonnen's bristle-haired nephew, said scornfully.

Paul looked back at the Emperor. "There's a Harkonnen with you. Give him a blade and let him come forward." He glared a challenge at Feyd.

"This is a Harkonnen animal," Gurney Hallack said. "Please, my lord, let me—"

Paul shook his head.

Chani pulled at Paul's arm. "Muad'Dib does not need to do this."

"But the Duke Paul must," Paul said. He took out his crysknife.

Feyd held the Emperor's own knife. The two young men circled warily, studying each other. Feyd moved skillfully. Paul tried to judge Feyd's weaknesses as he jabbed with his knife. Both fighters leaped and came close to striking deadly blows again and again, but they always missed. Their skills were well matched. Feyd led his attacks with his right hip. Paul wondered if he had a gom jabbar hidden there, in his clothing.

As Paul watched for the needle, Feyd bit his hand. Feyd laughed viciously.

Paul lunged at Feyd, but his move was slow, as if he were getting tired. Feyd danced away. He countered Paul's thrust, and kicked him to the ground. Chani cried out in fear.

Feyd smiled evilly, looking at Chani. "I'll make you mine, next," he said.

Paul leaped up and attacked Feyd furiously. He jabbed with his knife, and Feyd grabbed his arm. The two were locked in a clinch. Feyd tried to pull Paul toward the gom jabbar—but it was hidden on his *left* hip. Paul barely missed feeling the prick of the poisoned needle. As he twisted away, Feyd tripped him.

Feyd leaped on top of him. "You've seen your death now," Feyd hissed.

But then Paul heaved Feyd up and over his head. He had not been tiring at all. He had caught Feyd off guard. He held the other man down.

"You . . . you . . ." Feyd gasped, struggling to break free.

Paul's knife came down and killed him. Paul got to his feet, breathing hard. Rage still burned in him, as he thought of all the terrible things the Harkonnens had done to his family, and this world. He shouted once, using The Voice, and the floor beneath Feyd cracked open. Everything about the Harkonnens was evil and treacherous. But their evil was finished now.

"Muad'Dib no longer needs the weirding module. His voice alone is all powerful," a Fedaykin said. Everyone stared in disbelief.

Paul looked back at the Emperor. "I will tell you how it will be. I will marry your daughter, Princess Irulan. I will become the new Emperor."

"Only I sit on the throne!" said the Emperor.

"You'll have a throne on Salusa Secundus, your prison world," Paul answered. "Or else you will die." The Emperor kept silent.

Paul moved to Chani's side, seeing the grief on her face. He felt her pain in his own heart. No one had escaped the suffering his terrible purpose carried with it. Not even Chani, or himself. History was the greatest Maker of all, and it carried their human lives along on its back. "Chani, the Princess will have nothing of me but my name. You will be my real love forever, I promise you. Just as my mother was my father's only love."

He turned back to the others. Jessica put her arm around Chani, comforting her. She knew that Paul would be true to Chani, as his father had been true to her. And she knew that history would remember their love longer than it would remember Irulan.

Paul's sister Alia came forward with two Fremen monks. She lifted her hand, and one of the monks placed a rich cloak over Paul's shoulders.

Paul said to the Fremen, "You have the word of Muad'Dib. There will be justice in the galaxy. You will have Arrakis . . . Dune . . . your planet. There will be flowing water here, and rich green lands. But for the spice there will always be some desert. There will be fierce winds and trials to toughen men. We Fremen have a saying—" and he looked at the Reverend Mother Mohiam, "'God created Arrakis to train the faithful.' One cannot go against the word of God."

Everyone in the room stared at him silently. "Yes," Alia cried at last, "he *is* the Promised One, the Kwisatz Haderach!"

Paul's shining eyes were all blue, the color of the sunset sky beyond the windows of the palace. Outside, the sun was setting on the past. Tomorrow it would rise on a new future.

If you have enjoyed reading

The Dune™ Storybook,

you will also enjoy the great novels of the Dune Chronicles:

Dune

Dune Messiah

Children of Dune

God Emperor of Dune

Heretics of Dune

by Frank Herbert,
as well as

The Dune Encyclopedia

compiled by Willis E. McNelly.

All the above titles are available in
BERKLEY (paperback) and PUTNAM (hardcover) editions.